NAPPY HAIR

for Dr. Leo H. Kirchhoff
colleague and connection
Thank you for remembering me!
Carolivia Herron

by
Carolivia Herron

illustrated by **Joe Cepeda**

Alfred A. Knopf
New York

For Georgia Carol Johnson Herron and
Oscar Smith Herron, Sr.

My Beloved Parents
In our year of gold

Who accepted the awesome task,
and did not refuse to bring my nappy head
into the world.

We best be glad y'all had this chile.

—C. H.

For my father, José Perez Cepeda

—J. C.

THIS IS A BORZOI BOOK PUBLISHED BY ALFRED A. KNOPF, INC.

Text copyright © 1997 by Carolivia Herron
Illustrations copyright © 1997 by Joe Cepeda

Library of Congress Cataloging-in-Publication Data
Herron, Carolivia.
Nappy hair / by Carolivia Herron ; illustrated by Joe Cepeda.
p. cm.
Summary: Various people at a backyard picnic offer their comments on a young girl's
tightly curled, "nappy" hair.
ISBN 0-679-87937-4 (trade) — ISBN 0-679-97937-9 (lib. bdg.)
[1. Afro-Americans—Fiction. 2. Hair—Fiction.] I. Cepeda, Joe, ill. II. Title.
PZ7.H43225Nap 1997 96-2061
[E]—dc20

Printed in Mexico

10 9 8 7 6 5 4 3

Uncle Mordecai told this story
at the backyard picnic.
Uncle Mordecai told it,
the folks joined in between the lines,
little Jimmy taped it,
and here it is.

Brenda, you sure do got some nappy hair on
your head, don't you?
            Well.

It's your hair, Brenda, take the cake,
        Yep.

And come back and get the plate.
        Don't cha know.

It ain't easy to come by that kind of hair.

No, it ain't.

You just can't blame Africa. It's willful.

That's what it is.

Them some willful intentional naps you
got all over your head.

Sure enough.

Your hair intended to be nappy.

Indeed it did.

I mean combing your hair . . .

Yep.

. . . is like scrunching through the New Mexico
desert in brogans in the heat of summer.

That's the way.

It's like crunching through snow.

Y e p .

About a foot, two feet at least.

Uh-huh.

With two inches of crust on the top.

I can hear it.

Y'all know how it sounds when you
scrunching through snow like that?

I can hear it.

That's what her hair sounds like when
she comb it out in the morning.

Brother, you ought to be ashamed.

Ashamed? I'm not ashamed. I'm proud.
She's the only one in her school knows
how to talk right.

Ain't she something?

A rose among a thousand thorns.

I know it.

Them old hardheads think they can talk English.

Yep.

But this chile talks the king's English.

I hear her.

Talk the queen's English too.

She can do it.

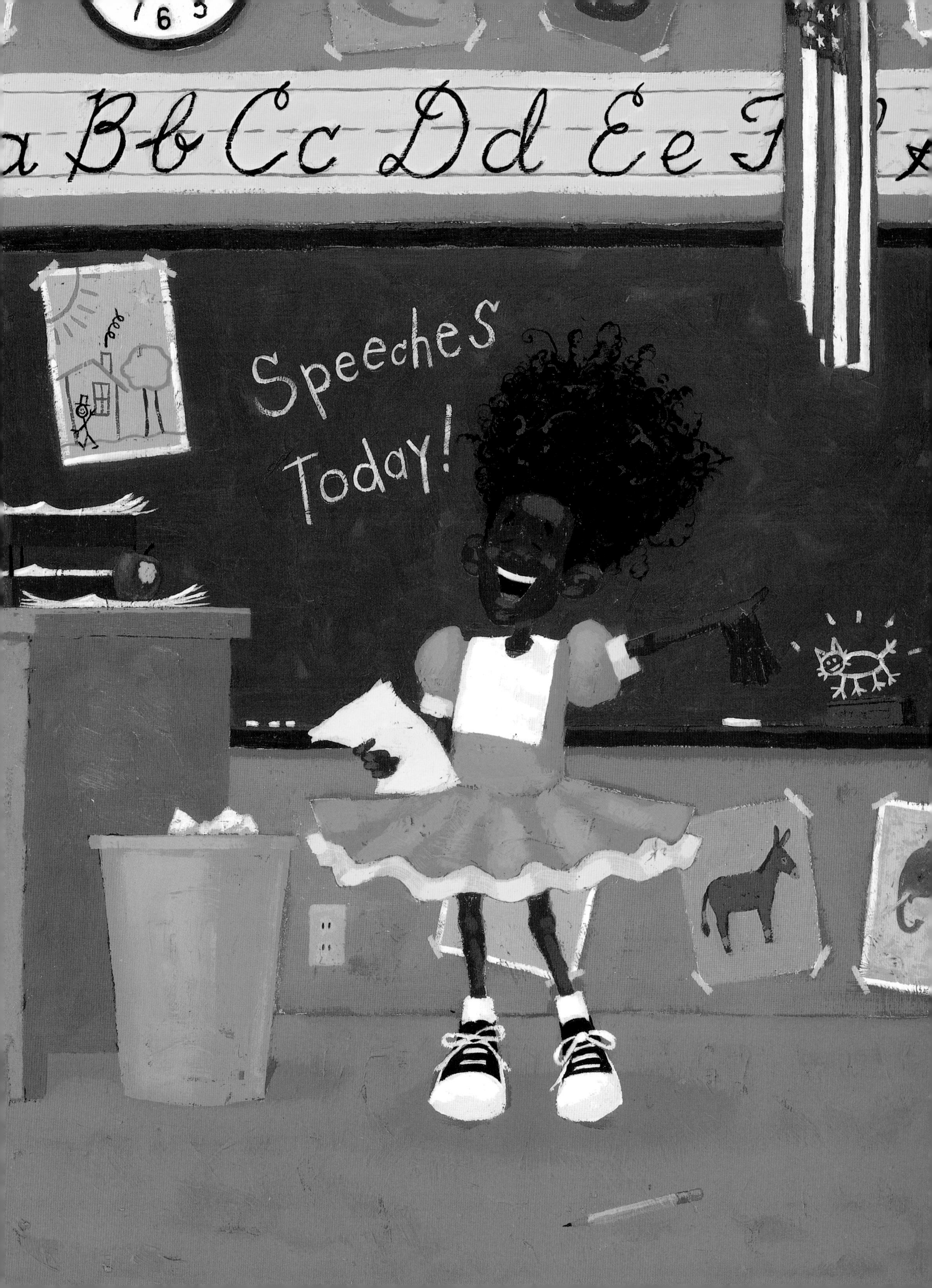

Speeches Today!

But she sure, Lord, got some nappy hair on her head.

Now, why's he got to come back to that?

And I'm gonna tell y'all how she came up with
all this nappy hair.

Brother, will you stop.

Her hair was an act of God.

Lord, listen to him now.

An act of God that came straight through Africa.

Well.

You see, the angels went up to God.

Oh, oh, here he goes.

Angels walk up to God to talk him out of it.

Will you listen to this?

Yep. They say, "Lord, Lord, Lord."

Well.

"Why you gotta be so mean, why you gotta be so willful,
why you gotta be so ornery, thinking about giving that nappy,
nappy hair to that innocent little child?"

Innocent.

"Sweet little girl like that, and you napping up her hair like you ain't got good sense."

That's what they said.

"Napping up her hair, five, six, seven, maybe eight complete circles per inch."

B r o t h e r .

I'm talking about eight complete
circles per inch of hair.

Please.

And the angels tryin' to talk him out of it.

Yep.

But God . . .

Well.

God wanted hisself some nappy hair
upon the face of the earth.

That's what it was.

So, God turn hisself around, look them angels square in the face.

Well.

And God say, "Get outta my way."

Yep.

He say, "This is my world."

It's the truth.

"This is my world, and this chile."

Well.

"This sweet little brown baby girl chile."

We hear you.

"She's going to have the nappiest hair in the world!"

That's what he said.

"Ain't going to be nothing they come up with going to straighten this chile's hair."

What you going to do?

"I'm talking about straightening combs."

Can it really be?

"I'm talking about relaxers and processes."

You said it.

"Ain't nothing going to straighten up the naps on this chile's head."

What you say!?

And it was done. *Ha!*

So here she come.

W e l l .

Sitting back in Africa making plans.

That's where it was.

Squinching her eyes and looking deep.

She was deep.

Getting ready to come to America
with them slaves.

Didn't we come over here?

Sold your momma for a nickel.

Yes, Lord, they did it.

And your daddy for a dime.

Yep.

I say they sold your momma for a buffalo.

That's the way it was.

And your daddy, they sold him for
one thin dime.

That's what they did.

But this nap come riding express,
coming on across the ocean from Africa,
wouldn't stop for nothing.

Didn't she come!

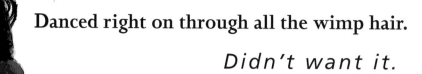

Danced right on through all the wimp hair.

Didn't want it.

Wouldn't stop, wouldn't mix,
wouldn't slow down for nobody.

Wouldn't do it.

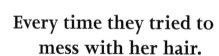

Every time they tried to
mess with her hair.

I can see it.

She stomped it, kicked it, snuck on around,
and came on through.

That's what she did.

Think she playing football, basketball,
or something.

Y e p .

Dribbling on down the line.

She's the one.

And when she was born,

We remember.

When we looked down on her in the cradle,
What did we see?

We all shout out and jump back.
Did we jump!

Laugh and shout, because I tell you she had
the kinkiest, the nappiest, the fuzziest, the most
screwed up, squeezed up, knotted up, tangled up,
twisted up, nappiest—I'm telling you, she had
the nappiest hair you've ever seen in your life.
That's what it was.

And the Lord.
W e l l .

The Lord in heaven.
What you say.

The Lord who brought the Israelites
out of Egypt.
Yes, he did.

He looked down on this cute little
brown baby girl.
He looked at her.

He looked at her and he say, "Well done."
Yep.

He say, "I got me one."

That's what he said.

"One nap of her hair is the only perfect circle in nature."

W e l l .

"I got me a cute little brown baby girl."
Keep talking.

"I got me at long last this cute little brown baby girl."
Well.

"And she's got the nappiest hair in the world."

Ain't it the truth.

Carolivia Herron

◎ **TARGET**®

Carolivia Herron

The Ides of March